MAD LIBS®

TOTALLY PINK
MAD LIBS

concept created by Roger Price and Leonard Stern

PSS!
PRICE STERN SLOAN
An Imprint of Penguin Group (USA) Inc.

W9-AAT-200

PRICE STERN SLOAN
Published by the Penguin Group
Penguin Group (USA) Inc., 375 Hudson Street, New York, New York 10014, USA
Penguin Group (Canada), 90 Eglinton Avenue East, Suite 700,
Toronto, Ontario M4P 2Y3, Canada
(a division of Pearson Penguin Canada Inc.)
Penguin Books Ltd., 80 Strand, London WC2R 0RL, England
Penguin Group Ireland, 25 St. Stephen's Green, Dublin 2, Ireland
(a division of Penguin Books Ltd.)
Penguin Group (Australia), 250 Camberwell Road, Camberwell, Victoria 3124, Australia
(a division of Pearson Australia Group Pty. Ltd.)
Penguin Books India Pvt. Ltd., 11 Community Centre,
Panchsheel Park, New Delhi—110 017, India
Penguin Group (NZ), 67 Apollo Drive, Rosedale, North Shore 0632, New Zealand
(a division of Pearson New Zealand Ltd.)
Penguin Books (South Africa) (Pty.) Ltd., 24 Sturdee Avenue,
Rosebank, Johannesburg 2196, South Africa

Penguin Books Ltd., Registered Offices:
80 Strand, London WC2R 0RL, England

Mad Libs format copyright © 2010 by Price Stern Sloan.

Published by Price Stern Sloan, a division of Penguin Young Readers Group,
345 Hudson Street, New York, New York 10014.

ISBN 978-0-8431-9898-0

3 5 7 9 10 8 6 4

MAD LIBS®
INSTRUCTIONS

MAD LIBS® is a game for people who don't like games!
It can be played by one, two, three, four, or forty.

● RIDICULOUSLY SIMPLE DIRECTIONS

In this tablet you will find stories containing blank spaces where words
are left out. One player, the READER, selects one of these stories. The
READER does not tell anyone what the story is about. Instead, he/she asks
the other players, the WRITERS, to give him/her words. These words are
used to fill in the blank spaces in the story.

● TO PLAY

The READER asks each WRITER in turn to call out a word—an adjective or
a noun or whatever the space calls for—and uses them to fill in the blank
spaces in the story. The result is a MAD LIBS® game.

When the READER then reads the completed MAD LIBS® game to the other
players, they will discover that they have written a story that is fantastic,
screamingly funny, shocking, silly, crazy, or just plain dumb—depending
upon which words each WRITER called out.

● EXAMPLE (*Before* and *After*)

" _____ !" he said _____
      EXCLAMATION   ADVERB

as he jumped into his convertible _____ and
                                                  NOUN

drove off with his _____ wife.
                           ADJECTIVE

" *Ouch* !" he said *stupidly*
      EXCLAMATION   ADVERB

as he jumped into his convertible *cat* and
                                                  NOUN

drove off with his *brave* wife.
                           ADJECTIVE

In case you have forgotten what adjectives, adverbs, nouns, and verbs are, here is a quick review:

An ADJECTIVE describes something or somebody. *Lumpy*, *soft*, *ugly*, *messy*, and *short* are adjectives.

An ADVERB tells how something is done. It modifies a verb and usually ends in "ly." *Modestly*, *stupidly*, *greedily*, and *carefully* are adverbs.

A NOUN is the name of a person, place, or thing. *Sidewalk*, *umbrella*, *bridle*, *bathtub*, and *nose* are nouns.

A VERB is an action word. *Run*, *pitch*, *jump*, and *swim* are verbs. Put the verbs in past tense if the directions say PAST TENSE. *Ran*, *pitched*, *jumped*, and *swam* are verbs in the past tense.

When we ask for A PLACE, we mean any sort of place: a country or city (*Spain*, *Cleveland*) or a room (*bathroom*, *kitchen*).

An EXCLAMATION or SILLY WORD is any sort of funny sound, gasp, grunt, or outcry, like *Wow!*, *Ouch!*, *Whomp!*, *Ick!*, and *Gadzooks!*

When we ask for specific words, like a NUMBER, a COLOR, an ANIMAL, or a PART OF THE BODY, we mean a word that is one of those things, like *seven*, *blue*, *horse*, or *head*.

When we ask for a PLURAL, it means more than one. For example, *cat* pluralized is *cats*.

MAD LIBS® is fun to play with friends, but you can also play it by yourself! To begin with, DO NOT look at the story on the page below. Fill in the blanks on this page with the words called for. Then, using the words you have selected, fill in the blank spaces in the story.

Now you've created your own hilarious MAD LIBS® game!

PINKTASTIC

NOUN _beach_

ADJECTIVE _garganchuas_

PART OF THE BODY (PLURAL) _feet_

VERB _run_

PLURAL NOUN _pens_

PLURAL NOUN _pillows_

PLURAL NOUN _beds_

ADJECTIVE _excited_

NUMBER _19_

ADJECTIVE _tired_

NOUN _book_

ADJECTIVE _red_

ADJECTIVE _happy_

NOUN _firework_

NOUN _grass_

MAD LIBS®
PINKTASTIC

My absolute favorite ___color___ in the whole, whole,
NOUN
___awesome___ world is pink. Everything I wear is pink,
ADJECTIVE
from my head down to my ___toes___. I eat, sleep, and
PART OF THE BODY (PLURAL)
___live___ pink! I redecorated my room with pink
VERB
wallpaper, pink carpeting, and pink ___furniture___. I cover
PLURAL NOUN
all my school ___projects___ in pink paper and use *only*
PLURAL NOUN
pink ___pens___ to write my homework. I even got
PLURAL NOUN
permission from the ___amazing___ principal to paint my
ADJECTIVE
locker pink! I can't wait until I turn ___16___ years old
NUMBER
and get my ___awesome___ license because I've been saving
ADJECTIVE
up money to buy a hot pink convertible ___ferarry___!
NOUN
It will be so ___cool___. Maybe one day I'll have
ADJECTIVE
a/an ___huge___ pink house, too! Then there will be no
ADJECTIVE
doubt in anyone's ___mind___ that pink is my favorite
NOUN
color in the whole, wide ___world___!
NOUN

MAD LIBS® is fun to play with friends, but you can also play it by yourself! To begin with, DO NOT look at the story on the page below. Fill in the blanks on this page with the words called for. Then, using the words you have selected, fill in the blank spaces in the story.

Now you've created your own hilarious MAD LIBS® game!

THE CUTEST BOY IN SCHOOL

PERSON IN ROOM (MALE) _____

ADJECTIVE _____

A PLACE _____

NOUN _____

ADJECTIVE _____

ADVERB _____

ADJECTIVE _____

NOUN _____

PART OF THE BODY _____

NOUN _____

SILLY WORD _____

NOUN _____

NOUN _____

NOUN _____

I cannot believe it: _____, the most
PERSON IN ROOM (MALE)

_____ boy in school, talked to me today! We were
ADJECTIVE

sitting in (the) _____, and he turned around and
A PLACE

asked to borrow my _____! At first I was so shocked
NOUN

I couldn't find the _____ words to respond—
ADJECTIVE

I just sat there staring at him _____. But then he
ADVERB

smiled his _____ smile, and I calmed down and
ADJECTIVE

reached into my _____ to get it for him. When he
NOUN

turned back around, I smacked myself in my _____.
PART OF THE BODY

He must have thought I was out of my _____. But
NOUN

when class was over, he didn't seem to think I was from planet

_____: He gave me back my _____
SILLY WORD NOUN

and walked me to _____ class! I hope he forgets his
NOUN

_____ and needs to borrow mine again tomorrow!
NOUN

MAD LIBS® is fun to play with friends, but you can also play it by yourself! To begin with, DO NOT look at the story on the page below. Fill in the blanks on this page with the words called for. Then, using the words you have selected, fill in the blank spaces in the story.

Now you've created your own hilarious MAD LIBS® game!

BESTIES 4 LIFE

NUMBER _____

NOUN _____

ADJECTIVE _____

ADJECTIVE _____

PLURAL NOUN _____

PLURAL NOUN _____

ADJECTIVE _____

A PLACE _____

CELEBRITY (MALE) _____

VERB _____

ADJECTIVE _____

ADJECTIVE _____

PLURAL NOUN _____

PLURAL NOUN _____

ADJECTIVE _____

MAD LIBS®

BESTIES 4 LIFE

I met my BFF when we were both _____ years old, and since
\qquad\qquad\qquad\quad NUMBER

then, we've been like two peas in a/an _____. We
\qquad\qquad\qquad\qquad\qquad\quad NOUN

met in drama class. She helped me learn my _____
\qquad\qquad\qquad\qquad\qquad\qquad ADJECTIVE

lines, and I taught her how to speak with a/an _____
\qquad\qquad\qquad\qquad\qquad\qquad\quad ADJECTIVE

accent. After class, we bonded over French _____
\qquad\qquad\qquad\qquad\qquad\qquad PLURAL NOUN

and milk shakes, which we both love! Back then we used to ride

our _____ around the neighborhood and play with
\quad PLURAL NOUN

_____ dolls, but now we spend our time shopping
\quad ADJECTIVE

at (the) _____ and watching movies starring
\qquad\qquad A PLACE

_____, our favorite actor. At weekend sleepovers,
CELEBRITY (MALE)

we _____ to our favorite music, read our
\qquad\quad VERB

_____ magazines, and talk about the _____
ADJECTIVE \qquad\qquad\qquad\qquad\qquad ADJECTIVE

boys we like at school. And we love to make chocolate chip

_____! We tell each other our deepest, darkest
\quad PLURAL NOUN

_____, and I know I can always count on her to be
\quad PLURAL NOUN

there! I'm lucky to have such a really _____ best friend.
\qquad\qquad\qquad\qquad\qquad\qquad ADJECTIVE

From TOTALLY PINK MAD LIBS® • Copyright © 2010 by Price Stern Sloan,
a division of Penguin Young Readers Group, 345 Hudson Street, New York, NY 10014.

MAD LIBS® is fun to play with friends, but you can also play it by yourself! To begin with, DO NOT look at the story on the page below. Fill in the blanks on this page with the words called for. Then, using the words you have selected, fill in the blank spaces in the story.

Now you've created your own hilarious MAD LIBS® game!

SCHOOL DANCE DOS AND DON'TS

ADJECTIVE _____

ADJECTIVE _____

ADJECTIVE _____

VERB _____

ADJECTIVE _____

PART OF THE BODY _____

ADJECTIVE _____

ADJECTIVE _____

PLURAL NOUN _____

CELEBRITY _____

NOUN _____

PERSON IN ROOM (MALE) _____

ADJECTIVE _____

VERB _____

PLURAL NOUN _____

MAD LIBS®
SCHOOL DANCE DOS
AND DON'TS

School dances sure can be a lot of fun if you just follow these

_____ tips:
ADJECTIVE

DO get ready with your _____ friends.
ADJECTIVE

Play _____ music while you get in the mood to
ADJECTIVE

_____ all night long!
VERB

DON'T worry about being a/an _____
ADJECTIVE

dancer. Just let your _____ down and have a/an
PART OF THE BODY

_____ time, and you'll look great!
ADJECTIVE

DO bust out in a/an _____ choreographed dance
ADJECTIVE

with your best _____ the moment your favorite
PLURAL NOUN

_____ song comes on.
CELEBRITY

DON'T ask the DJ to dedicate a/an _____ to
NOUN

your crush, _____, unless you're really sure he has
PERSON IN ROOM (MALE)

_____ feelings for you, too.
ADJECTIVE

DO get up the nerve to ask a boy to _____. They love
VERB

_____ with confidence!
PLURAL NOUN

MAD LIBS® is fun to play with friends, but you can also play it by yourself! To begin with, DO NOT look at the story on the page below. Fill in the blanks on this page with the words called for. Then, using the words you have selected, fill in the blank spaces in the story.

Now you've created your own hilarious MAD LIBS® game!

IDK Y PPL R LOLING

ADJECTIVE _____

PERSON IN ROOM (FEMALE) _____

PERSON IN ROOM (FEMALE) _____

PERSON IN ROOM (MALE) _____

ADJECTIVE _____

NOUN _____

ADJECTIVE _____

ADJECTIVE _____

LETTER OF THE ALPHABET _____

NOUN _____

NOUN _____

NOUN _____

ADJECTIVE _____

NUMBER _____

NOUN _____

MAD LIBS®

IDK Y PPL R LOLING

A/An _____ text message conversation to be read by
 ADJECTIVE

_____ and _____.
 PERSON IN ROOM (FEMALE)   PERSON IN ROOM (FEMALE)

Girl 1: i heard that _____ is going 2 B at ur party
 PERSON IN ROOM (MALE)

2morrow!

Girl 2: R U serious??? he is so _____—i can't believe
 ADJECTIVE

he even wants 2 be at my _____!
 NOUN

Girl 1: there's _____ gossip going around that he
 ADJECTIVE

has a/an _____ crush on U, and wants 2 ask U to go
 ADJECTIVE

out with him!

Girl 2: O-M-_____! it's a/an _____
 LETTER OF THE ALPHABET   NOUN

come true! this will B the gr8st _____ ever!
 NOUN

Girl 1: i know! U R such a lucky _____. U guys will
 NOUN

B the most _____ couple!
 ADJECTIVE

Girl 2: def!! i have to make sure there are at least _____
 NUMBER

love songs on my playlist! :) C U 2morrow nite!

Girl 1: l8r, you lucky _____, you!
 NOUN

MAD LIBS® is fun to play with friends, but you can also play it by yourself! To begin with, DO NOT look at the story on the page below. Fill in the blanks on this page with the words called for. Then, using the words you have selected, fill in the blank spaces in the story.

Now you've created your own hilarious MAD LIBS® game!

A ROCKIN' NIGHT

ADJECTIVE _____

VERB _____

NOUN _____

NUMBER _____

ADJECTIVE _____

PART OF THE BODY (PLURAL) _____

PERSON IN ROOM (MALE) _____

PERSON IN ROOM (MALE) _____

CELEBRITY (MALE) _____

VERB _____

EXCLAMATION _____

VERB (PAST TENSE) _____

ADJECTIVE _____

ADJECTIVE _____

ADJECTIVE _____

MAD LIBS

A ROCKIN' NIGHT

I got to see my favorite band, the _____ Boys,

ADJECTIVE

_____ live in concert tonight! I won two front-row
VERB

tickets by calling in to the local radio _____ and

NOUN

being caller number _____. I couldn't believe my

NUMBER

_____ luck! So my best friend and I arrived at the
ADJECTIVE

sold-out show and screamed our _____ off when

PART OF THE BODY (PLURAL)

the band stepped onstage. We danced and sang along while

_____, _____, and
PERSON IN ROOM (MALE)   PERSON IN ROOM (MALE)

_____ rocked out only ten feet in front of us! Then,
CELEBRITY (MALE)

during my favorite song, "Girl, I Wanna _____ with

VERB

You," the band pulled us up onstage! _____! We

EXCLAMATION

_____ in front of the whole crowd and got to sing
VERB (PAST TENSE)

alongside the _____ Boys! And that's not all. When

ADJECTIVE

the show was over, they asked us to be in their next

_____ video! Can you believe it? Me neither! It was
ADJECTIVE

the most _____ night of my life!

ADJECTIVE

MAD LIBS® is fun to play with friends, but you can also play it by yourself! To begin with, DO NOT look at the story on the page below. Fill in the blanks on this page with the words called for. Then, using the words you have selected, fill in the blank spaces in the story.

Now you've created your own hilarious MAD LIBS® game!

MADEMOISELLE FLOOFY

ADJECTIVE _____

SILLY WORD _____

ANIMAL _____

PLURAL NOUN _____

NUMBER _____

NOUN _____

ADJECTIVE _____

VERB _____

PART OF THE BODY (PLURAL) _____

PLURAL NOUN _____

ANIMAL _____

SILLY WORD _____

ADJECTIVE _____

NOUN _____

PART OF THE BODY (PLURAL) _____

NOUN _____

MAD LIBS

MADEMOISELLE FLOOFY

I have the most _____ pet ever: Mademoiselle Floofy
                     ADJECTIVE

von _____! She's a beautiful _____
        SILLY WORD   ANIMAL

with long, floppy _____. I got Mademoiselle
                        PLURAL NOUN

Floofy when she was _____ months old. She was
                            NUMBER

so tiny! I worked hard training her, and now she is completely

_____-broken and knows a lot of highly imaginative,
        NOUN

_____ tricks. She can sit and _____,
   ADJECTIVE   VERB

and she knows how to dance on her back _____.
                                            PART OF THE BODY (PLURAL)

Mademoiselle Floofy loves to eat _____, and she'll do
                                     PLURAL NOUN

anything to get some! Her best friend, a/an _____
                                                ANIMAL

named Marilyn Mon-_____, lives across the street,
                        SILLY WORD

and I take them both to the _____ park to play when
                                 ADJECTIVE

it's nice outside. And at night when I read a/an _____
                                                    NOUN

in bed, Mademoiselle Floofy curls up on my _____
                                                PART OF THE BODY (PLURAL)

and falls fast asleep. She's the best _____ a girl could
                                          NOUN

ever want!

From TOTALLY PINK MAD LIBS® • Copyright © 2010 by Price Stern Sloan,
a division of Penguin Young Readers Group, 345 Hudson Street, New York, NY 10014.

MAD LIBS® is fun to play with friends, but you can also play it by yourself! To begin with, DO NOT look at the story on the page below. Fill in the blanks on this page with the words called for. Then, using the words you have selected, fill in the blank spaces in the story.

Now you've created your own hilarious MAD LIBS® game!

SPA DAY!

PLURAL NOUN _____

ADJECTIVE _____

PLURAL NOUN _____

TYPE OF LIQUID _____

ADJECTIVE _____

PART OF THE BODY (PLURAL) _____

PLURAL NOUN _____

PLURAL NOUN _____

ADJECTIVE _____

A PLACE _____

ADJECTIVE _____

COLOR _____

COLOR _____

PLURAL NOUN _____

ADJECTIVE _____

NUMBER _____

MAD LIBS®
SPA DAY!

Once a month, my _____ and I go to the
                        PLURAL NOUN

_____ salon and have a spa day. We sit in
ADJECTIVE

massaging _____ and soak our feet in tubs of
              PLURAL NOUN

_____ to relax. Then _____
TYPE OF LIQUID   ADJECTIVE

masseuses go to work kneading our _____. It's
                                    PART OF THE BODY (PLURAL)

so soothing! You feel all of your _____ melting
                                    PLURAL NOUN

away. Next they put masks made of _____
                                     PLURAL NOUN

on our faces; they're supposed to make your skin look soft

and more _____. After that we head to (the)
            ADJECTIVE

_____ to get manicures and pedicures. They
A PLACE

cut and file our nails, then paint them in _____
                                              ADJECTIVE

polishes like _____ or _____.
                 COLOR   COLOR

  Finally, we get our _____ cut and styled like
                         PLURAL NOUN

the most _____ celebrities, and we all feel like
            ADJECTIVE

_____ dollars!
NUMBER

MAD LIBS® is fun to play with friends, but you can also play it by yourself! To begin with, DO NOT look at the story on the page below. Fill in the blanks on this page with the words called for. Then, using the words you have selected, fill in the blank spaces in the story.

Now you've created your own hilarious MAD LIBS® game!

HE LOVES ME . . .

PERSON IN ROOM (FEMALE) _____

A PLACE _____

ADJECTIVE _____

NOUN _____

ADJECTIVE _____

ADJECTIVE _____

ADJECTIVE _____

COLOR _____

ADJECTIVE _____

NOUN _____

PLURAL NOUN _____

ADJECTIVE _____

NOUN _____

PLURAL NOUN _____

ADJECTIVE _____

NOUN _____

NOUN _____

MAD LIBS

HE LOVES ME...

Dear _____: I see you a lot in (the) _____
    PERSON IN ROOM (FEMALE)   A PLACE

and I think you're really _____. I wrote you this
                              ADJECTIVE

_____ to tell you how I feel about you.
        NOUN

Roses are _____, violets are blue.
              ADJECTIVE

I think you're _____ and very _____, too.
                    ADJECTIVE   ADJECTIVE

Violets are _____, clover is green,
                  COLOR

You're the most _____ _____ I've
                      ADJECTIVE   NOUN

ever seen.

_____ are yellow, roses are red.
    PLURAL NOUN

You're _____ from your toes to the top of your
            ADJECTIVE

_____.
      NOUN

Roses are red, _____ are black.
                    PLURAL NOUN

I like you—do you like me back?

I think you're so _____, I want you to know.
                      ADJECTIVE

Will you please be my _____? Check here:
                            NOUN

_____ or no.
      NOUN

MAD LIBS® is fun to play with friends, but you can also play it by yourself! To begin with, DO NOT look at the story on the page below. Fill in the blanks on this page with the words called for. Then, using the words you have selected, fill in the blank spaces in the story.

Now you've created your own hilarious MAD LIBS® game!

. . . SHE LOVES ME NOT

FIRST NAME (MALE) _____

ADJECTIVE _____

ADVERB _____

ADJECTIVE _____

PLURAL NOUN _____

ADJECTIVE _____

VERB _____

NOUN _____

NOUN _____

ADJECTIVE _____

ADJECTIVE _____

ANIMAL _____

NUMBER _____

NOUN _____

PERSON IN ROOM (MALE) _____

MAD LIBS®

... SHE LOVES ME NOT

Dear _____: Thank you for the _____
　　　　FIRST NAME (MALE)　　　　　　　　　　　　　　ADJECTIVE

poem you sent me. It was _____ the most
　　　　　　　　　　　　　　　　ADVERB

_____ present I've ever gotten. You have
ADJECTIVE

such a way with _____! I think you're
　　　　　　　　　　PLURAL NOUN

a very _____ boy, and maybe we could
　　　　　　ADJECTIVE

_____ together sometime but, unfortunately, I
　　VERB

can't be your _____. It's not you, it's my
　　　　　　　　　　NOUN

_____. You see, I already have a/an
　　NOUN

_____ boyfriend. We like a lot of the same
ADJECTIVE

things, like watching _____ movies and
　　　　　　　　　　　　　ADJECTIVE

_____-back riding. We've been dating for
ANIMAL

_____ days, and I think he may be "the one." So
NUMBER

thank you again for your poetic _____, and I hope
　　　　　　　　　　　　　　　　NOUN

you find someone who makes you as happy as _____
　　　　　　　　　　　　　　　　　　　　　　PERSON IN ROOM (MALE)

makes me!

MAD LIBS® is fun to play with friends, but you can also play it by yourself! To begin with, DO NOT look at the story on the page below. Fill in the blanks on this page with the words called for. Then, using the words you have selected, fill in the blank spaces in the story.

Now you've created your own hilarious MAD LIBS® game!

SING IT, SISTERS!

PLURAL NOUN _____

ADJECTIVE _____

PLURAL NOUN _____

ADJECTIVE _____

NOUN _____

ADJECTIVE _____

NOUN _____

A PLACE _____

VERB _____

ADJECTIVE _____

PLURAL NOUN _____

NOUN _____

A PLACE _____

VERB _____

MAD LIBS®
SING IT, SISTERS!

If one of your _____ has a karaoke birthday party,
_____ PLURAL NOUN

do you know what _____ songs you would sing?
_____ ADJECTIVE

You should always be prepared! Maybe the classic

"_____ Just Want to Have Fun" is your style.
_____ PLURAL NOUN

Or what about "Born to Be _____"? There's also
_____ ADJECTIVE

the ever-popular "Livin' on a/an _____," but
_____ NOUN

you'll have to be able to hit some pretty _____
_____ ADJECTIVE

notes for that one! If you want to go with something newer,

both "You Belong with _____" and "Party in
_____ NOUN

(the) _____" are really fun to sing. And if you like
_____ A PLACE

to dance while you're singing, "Twist and _____" is
_____ VERB

a/an _____ choice. If you want a surefire hit,
_____ ADJECTIVE

"Single _____ (Put a/an _____ on
_____ PLURAL NOUN _____ NOUN

It)" would work. But my favorite karaoke song will always be

"Sweet Home (the) _____" because everyone knows
_____ A PLACE

the words and will _____ along!
_____ VERB

MAD LIBS® is fun to play with friends, but you can also play it by yourself! To begin with, DO NOT look at the story on the page below. Fill in the blanks on this page with the words called for. Then, using the words you have selected, fill in the blank spaces in the story.

Now you've created your own hilarious MAD LIBS® game!

ARE YOU HIP TO THE JIVE?

NUMBER _____

ADJECTIVE _____

SAME ADJECTIVE _____

SILLY WORD _____

ADJECTIVE _____

ADJECTIVE _____

NOUN _____

NOUN _____

ADVERB _____

SAME ADVERB _____

ADJECTIVE _____

PART OF THE BODY _____

MAD LIBS

ARE YOU HIP TO THE JIVE?

Do you have the 4-1-_____ on the latest slang? Are
                        NUMBER
you _____? For instance, "_____"
        ADJECTIVE   SAME ADJECTIVE
means "trendy." If you call someone a/an "_____," it's
                                          SILLY WORD
another way of saying you think that person is a cutie. If

something is totally _____, you might say it's
                        ADJECTIVE
"_____." And when you call someone a/an
        ADJECTIVE
"_____," you mean that they are totally lame. On
        NOUN
the other hand, if someone is extremely cool, you might say, "Hey,

that guy's a total _____!" And any time you hear
                    NOUN
someone use the word "_____," it means "very" or
                        ADVERB
"extremely": "That outfit is _____ awesome!" Just
                            SAME ADVERB
don't use these words all at once, or no one will be able to

understand a/an _____ word that comes out of
                ADJECTIVE
your _____!
        PART OF THE BODY

MAD LIBS® is fun to play with friends, but you can also play it by yourself! To begin with, DO NOT look at the story on the page below. Fill in the blanks on this page with the words called for. Then, using the words you have selected, fill in the blank spaces in the story.

Now you've created your own hilarious MAD LIBS® game!

DEAR DIARY

VERB ENDING IN "ING" _____

ADJECTIVE _____

NUMBER _____

NOUN _____

ADJECTIVE _____

ADJECTIVE _____

VERB _____

PLURAL NOUN _____

VERB (PAST TENSE) _____

ADJECTIVE _____

SILLY WORD _____

NOUN _____

ADVERB _____

PLURAL NOUN _____

ADJECTIVE _____

ADJECTIVE _____

EXCLAMATION _____

ADJECTIVE _____

MAD LIBS®
DEAR DIARY

Dear Diary: Today I tried out for the cheer-_____

_____ VERB ENDING IN "ING"

squad. I've been practicing my _____ roundoffs and

_____ ADJECTIVE

cheers for weeks! My favorite cheer is "One, two, three,

_____—your _____ will never score! Five, six,

NUMBER   NOUN

seven, eight—because our team is really _____!" At

_____ ADJECTIVE

the tryouts, they taught us a dance routine and we learned some

_____ new cheers. Then we had to _____

ADJECTIVE   VERB

in front of a panel of _____. I was so nervous! I danced

_____ PLURAL NOUN

and _____ and did some _____ handsprings.

VERB (PAST TENSE)   ADJECTIVE

Then I pulled out my big surprise: a jump I made up called the

_____! I took a deep _____, went for it,

SILLY WORD   NOUN

and landed it _____! The judges loved it. They don't

_____ ADVERB

post the official _____ until tomorrow, but before I

_____ PLURAL NOUN

left, the coach gave me a/an _____ wink and said,

_____ ADJECTIVE

"_____ job!" _____! I'm really going to be

ADJECTIVE   EXCLAMATION

a/an _____ cheerleader!

ADJECTIVE

From TOTALLY PINK MAD LIBS® • Copyright © 2010 by Price Stern Sloan,
a division of Penguin Young Readers Group, 345 Hudson Street, New York, NY 10014.

MAD LIBS® is fun to play with friends, but you can also play it by yourself! To begin with, DO NOT look at the story on the page below. Fill in the blanks on this page with the words called for. Then, using the words you have selected, fill in the blank spaces in the story.

Now you've created your own hilarious MAD LIBS® game!

SASSY SISTERS

NOUN _____

PLURAL NOUN _____

ADJECTIVE _____

VERB _____

ADJECTIVE _____

PLURAL NOUN _____

PLURAL NOUN _____

NOUN _____

NUMBER _____

ADJECTIVE _____

ADJECTIVE _____

ADJECTIVE _____

NOUN _____

NOUN _____

MAD LIBS®
SASSY SISTERS

Sister 1: My younger _____ and I are best friends!
<u>NOUN</u>

We have the same taste in _____ (we only like the
<u>PLURAL NOUN</u>

_____ kind), and we both love to _____.
<u>ADJECTIVE</u>   <u>VERB</u>

Sister 2: Yeah, but we do have _____ fights sometimes.
<u>ADJECTIVE</u>

Mostly over whose _____ are whose.
<u>PLURAL NOUN</u>

Sister 1: She does like to take my _____, although
<u>PLURAL NOUN</u>

she calls it "borrowing." But it's okay because I "borrow" her

_____ sometimes when she's not around.
<u>NOUN</u>

Sister 2: What?? I have asked you _____ times not to
<u>NUMBER</u>

touch my _____ things!
<u>ADJECTIVE</u>

Sister 1: Sorry! But we really do love each other. We're so

_____ to have each other. I couldn't ask for a more
<u>ADJECTIVE</u>

_____ sister.
<u>ADJECTIVE</u>

Sister 2: I really do have the best older _____ in the
<u>NOUN</u>

world. (Even if she does think she's the greatest thing since sliced

_____!)
<u>NOUN</u>

From TOTALLY PINK MAD LIBS® • Copyright © 2010 by Price Stern Sloan,
a division of Penguin Young Readers Group, 345 Hudson Street, New York, NY 10014.

MAD LIBS® is fun to play with friends, but you can also play it by yourself! To begin with, DO NOT look at the story on the page below. Fill in the blanks on this page with the words called for. Then, using the words you have selected, fill in the blank spaces in the story.

Now you've created your own hilarious MAD LIBS® game!

HOW TO THROW A PARTY

PLURAL NOUN _____

ADJECTIVE _____

NUMBER _____

ADJECTIVE _____

PLURAL NOUN _____

NOUN _____

ADJECTIVE _____

PERSON IN ROOM (MALE) _____

ADJECTIVE _____

VERB _____

ADJECTIVE _____

NOUN _____

PLURAL NOUN _____

ADJECTIVE _____

ADJECTIVE _____

NOUN _____

PART OF THE BODY _____

ADVERB _____

NOUN _____

MAD LIBS®
HOW TO THROW A PARTY

Here is a list of _____ to make throwing a/an
                          PLURAL NOUN

_____ party as easy as one, two, _____!
   ADJECTIVE   NUMBER

1. _____ Food. Choose things that everyone likes to eat,
      ADJECTIVE

like pizza or fried _____. And make sure you have an
                        PLURAL NOUN

assortment of _____ soda to drink!
                   NOUN

2. The Right Music. You'll want to pick songs that are

_____. Try to select bands that everyone knows, like
   ADJECTIVE

the _____ Band or the _____ Dolls. Most
       PERSON IN ROOM (MALE)   ADJECTIVE

importantly, choose music that's easy to _____ to!
                                              VERB

3. _____ Décor. Making the _____ look right is a
      ADJECTIVE   NOUN

big part of the night! Hang lots of _____ from the ceilings
                                        PLURAL NOUN

and walls, and have _____ favors for everyone.
                         ADJECTIVE

4. The Perfect Guest List. Of course your _____ friends have
                                               ADJECTIVE

to be there, and maybe even the cute _____ you've had
                                          NOUN

your _____ on in school! Just make sure your guests all get
      PART OF THE BODY

along _____—a fight could really ruin your _____!
         ADVERB   NOUN

From TOTALLY PINK MAD LIBS® • Copyright © 2010 by Price Stern Sloan,
a division of Penguin Young Readers Group, 345 Hudson Street, New York, NY 10014.

MAD LIBS® is fun to play with friends, but you can also play it by yourself! To begin with, DO NOT look at the story on the page below. Fill in the blanks on this page with the words called for. Then, using the words you have selected, fill in the blank spaces in the story.

Now you've created your own hilarious MAD LIBS® game!

A ROYAL FAIRY TALE (PART ONE)

ADJECTIVE _____

NOUN _____

ADJECTIVE _____

VERB ENDING IN "ING" _____

PLURAL NOUN _____

ADJECTIVE _____

PLURAL NOUN _____

ADJECTIVE _____

NOUN _____

A PLACE _____

SAME PLACE _____

SAME PLACE _____

ADJECTIVE _____

NOUN _____

PLURAL NOUN _____

MAD LIBS
A ROYAL FAIRY TALE
(PART ONE)

Today was the most _____ day of my entire life! When
                        ADJECTIVE

I woke up this morning, I was a regular _____ like
                                        NOUN

everyone else. But then I found out a/an _____ secret.
                                         ADJECTIVE

I was _____ through the closet where my mom
      VERB ENDING IN "ING"

keeps all of our _____ and I found a baby picture
                 PLURAL NOUN

of me wearing a shiny, _____ tiara. When I asked my
                       ADJECTIVE

_____ why they had dressed me up like that, they
PLURAL NOUN

finally told me the _____ truth: I'm actually a royal
                    ADJECTIVE

_____! It turns out that my dad is the son of the king
NOUN

of (the) _____, which makes him the *prince* of (the)
         A PLACE

_____ and me the *princess* of (the) _____.
SAME PLACE   SAME PLACE

My parents moved here to get away from the _____
                                           ADJECTIVE

life, but they say I have the right to live my life like a true

_____ if I want to. And do I want to? You bet your
NOUN

_____ I do!
PLURAL NOUN

MAD LIBS® is fun to play with friends, but you can also play it by yourself! To begin with, DO NOT look at the story on the page below. Fill in the blanks on this page with the words called for. Then, using the words you have selected, fill in the blank spaces in the story.

Now you've created your own hilarious MAD LIBS® game!

A ROYAL FAIRY TALE (PART TWO)

NOUN _____

ADVERB _____

ADJECTIVE _____

NOUN _____

NOUN _____

PLURAL NOUN _____

NOUN _____

ADJECTIVE _____

CELEBRITY (MALE) _____

PERSON IN ROOM (FEMALE) _____

ADJECTIVE _____

ADJECTIVE _____

ADJECTIVE _____

NOUN _____

NOUN _____

ADJECTIVE _____

FIRST NAME (MALE) _____

ADJECTIVE _____

PERSON IN ROOM (MALE) _____

A PLACE _____

Now that I know I'm a royal _____, I'm going to live
                                    NOUN

_____. I'm not going to ride my _____
        ADVERB   ADJECTIVE

bike to school anymore; I'll have a driver pick me up in a stretch

_____ instead! And I'll never have to take out the
        NOUN

_____ or wash the _____ again! Maybe the
        NOUN   PLURAL NOUN

mayor will ask me to cut the _____ at the dedication
                                        NOUN

of our new _____ building. And since _____
                ADJECTIVE   CELEBRITY (MALE)

and _____ are both subjects of my country,
        PERSON IN ROOM (FEMALE)

I might even get to invite them as my _____ guests for
                                                ADJECTIVE

a/an _____ dinner! I'll ride on the _____
            ADJECTIVE   ADJECTIVE

float in the _____ Day Parade, sing the "_____
                    NOUN   NOUN

-Spangled Banner" at the _____ Bowl, and even
                                    ADJECTIVE

give a speech at the _____ Awards! But the best
                            FIRST NAME (MALE)

part is that maybe I'll get to marry the _____ Prince
                                                ADJECTIVE

_____ of (the) _____ in a fancy, royal
PERSON IN ROOM (MALE)   A PLACE

wedding!

MAD LIBS® is fun to play with friends, but you can also play it by yourself! To begin with, DO NOT look at the story on the page below. Fill in the blanks on this page with the words called for. Then, using the words you have selected, fill in the blank spaces in the story.

Now you've created your own hilarious MAD LIBS® game!

THE PERFECT OUTFIT

PERSON IN ROOM (FEMALE) _____

ADJECTIVE _____

NOUN _____

ADJECTIVE _____

NOUN _____

ADJECTIVE _____

PLURAL NOUN _____

ADJECTIVE _____

ADJECTIVE _____

NOUN _____

PART OF THE BODY (PLURAL) _____

ADJECTIVE _____

ADJECTIVE _____

ADJECTIVE _____

ADVERB _____

NOUN _____

MAD LIBS®

THE PERFECT OUTFIT

When you and your BFF, _____, go out to a/an
PERSON IN ROOM (FEMALE)

_____ party or even a football _____,
ADJECTIVE NOUN

you have to look your _____ best. And, of course,
ADJECTIVE

you'll need the perfect _____ for every occasion.
NOUN

The right pair of pants is a/an _____ start. You'll
ADJECTIVE

always look classic in a pair of denim _____.
PLURAL NOUN

Or you may want to dress up in a/an _____ skirt.
ADJECTIVE

Once that is decided, it's time to pick a/an _____
ADJECTIVE

shirt. It should always flatter your _____ and
NOUN

make your _____ look _____. Then
PART OF THE BODY (PLURAL) ADJECTIVE

the shoes: sporty or _____, heels or flats? Finally,
ADJECTIVE

_____ jewelry and the right hairstyle will make
ADJECTIVE

your outfit stand out _____! With the perfect outfit
ADVERB

assembled, you're ready to take on the _____!
NOUN

From TOTALLY PINK MAD LIBS® • Copyright © 2010 by Price Stern Sloan,
a division of Penguin Young Readers Group, 345 Hudson Street, New York, NY 10014.

MAD LIBS® is fun to play with friends, but you can also play it by yourself! To begin with, DO NOT look at the story on the page below. Fill in the blanks on this page with the words called for. Then, using the words you have selected, fill in the blank spaces in the story.

Now you've created your own hilarious MAD LIBS® game!

TRUTH OR DARE

PLURAL NOUN _____

PERSON IN ROOM (FEMALE) _____

NOUN _____

VERB (PAST TENSE) _____

A PLACE _____

ADJECTIVE _____

PERSON IN ROOM (FEMALE) _____

ADJECTIVE _____

ADJECTIVE _____

PERSON IN ROOM (MALE) _____

NOUN _____

NOUN _____

SAME NOUN _____

MAD LIBS®

TRUTH OR DARE

At my BFF's last party, my _____ and I played Truth
                                    PLURAL NOUN

or Dare. First I chose Truth, and _____ asked
                                         PERSON IN ROOM (FEMALE)

me what my most embarrassing _____ was. I had
                                          NOUN

to admit it was at summer camp when I _____
                                              VERB (PAST TENSE)

in (the) _____. I know it must sound totally
            A PLACE

_____ to everyone else, but I was embarrassed
   ADJECTIVE

all over again! So the next time I chose Dare instead. My friend

_____ dared me to go into her _____
PERSON IN ROOM (FEMALE)   ADJECTIVE

brother's room, sing "I'm a/an _____ Teapot," and
                                      ADJECTIVE

tell him I had a crush on _____. And I did it!
                              PERSON IN ROOM (MALE)

Strangely enough, her _____ was so embarrassed,
                            NOUN

he ran out of the room. From now on in Truth or Dare, it's the

_____ and nothing but the _____
   NOUN   SAME NOUN

for me!

MAD LIBS® is fun to play with friends, but you can also play it by yourself! To begin with, DO NOT look at the story on the page below. Fill in the blanks on this page with the words called for. Then, using the words you have selected, fill in the blank spaces in the story.

Now you've created your own hilarious MAD LIBS® game!

SHOPPING SPREE!

SILLY WORD _____

NUMBER _____

A PLACE _____

ADJECTIVE _____

NUMBER _____

ADJECTIVE _____

ARTICLE OF CLOTHING (PLURAL) _____

PLURAL NOUN _____

PLURAL NOUN _____

PLURAL NOUN _____

PERSON IN ROOM (MALE) _____

COLOR _____

NOUN _____

NOUN _____

ADJECTIVE _____

A PLACE _____

MAD LIBS®

SHOPPING SPREE!

_____! You've just won a/an _____-dollar
<u>SILLY WORD</u>   <u>NUMBER</u>

shopping spree at (the) _____! What will you buy
                        <u>A PLACE</u>

with all that _____ money?
              <u>ADJECTIVE</u>

- a/an _____-inch television for your bedroom
       <u>NUMBER</u>

- a/an _____ new wardrobe, complete with
       <u>ADJECTIVE</u>

  _____, _____, and the
  <u>ARTICLE OF CLOTHING (PLURAL)</u>   <u>PLURAL NOUN</u>

  hottest _____
          <u>PLURAL NOUN</u>

- enough chocolate-covered _____ to last your
                           <u>PLURAL NOUN</u>

  whole life

- a lifetime pass to the _____ World theme
                         <u>PERSON IN ROOM (MALE)</u>

  parks

- tickets to see your favorite band, _____
                                     <u>COLOR</u>

  Day, at every stop on their _____-wide tour—
                              <u>NOUN</u>

  and your own private _____ to take you there
                       <u>NOUN</u>

- your own _____ castle off the coast of (the)
           <u>ADJECTIVE</u>

  _____
  <u>A PLACE</u>

MAD LIBS® is fun to play with friends, but you can also play it by yourself! To begin with, DO NOT look at the story on the page below. Fill in the blanks on this page with the words called for. Then, using the words you have selected, fill in the blank spaces in the story.

Now you've created your own hilarious MAD LIBS® game!

TOTALLY PINK MAKEOVER

ADJECTIVE _____

ADJECTIVE _____

PART OF THE BODY (PLURAL) _____

PLURAL NOUN _____

ADJECTIVE _____

ADJECTIVE _____

PART OF THE BODY _____

NOUN _____

ADJECTIVE _____

NOUN _____

ADJECTIVE _____

PLURAL NOUN _____

PART OF THE BODY (PLURAL) _____

MAD LIBS®
TOTALLY PINK MAKEOVER

Are your clothes _____ and old-fashioned?
ADJECTIVE

Do you need a new, _____ look? It's time for
ADJECTIVE

a totally pink makeover! You'll sparkle from your head to your

_____.
PART OF THE BODY (PLURAL)

1. Clothes: Make sure to wear _____ that are either sparkly
PLURAL NOUN

   or pink. They should make you confident and _____.
ADJECTIVE

2. Makeup: The more _____ and shimmery, the better!
ADJECTIVE

   Glittery eye shadow and shiny _____ gloss will
PART OF THE BODY

   make you twinkle like the _____ you are!
NOUN

3. Hair: A/An _____ haircut is crucial to a good makeover.
ADJECTIVE

   Try to change it up: If you've been wearing your _____
NOUN

   long lately, try a shorter cut. If it's all one length, bangs could

   make you look _____!
ADJECTIVE

4. Accessories: Find the right purses, jewelry, and _____
PLURAL NOUN

   to match your new look.

Wow! The new you should be turning _____ left
PART OF THE BODY (PLURAL)

and right!

This book is published by

PSS!
PRICE STERN SLOAN

whose other splendid titles include
such literary classics as

Best of Mad Libs®	Mad Libs® in Love
Camp Daze Mad Libs®	Mad Libs® on the Road
Christmas Carol Mad Libs®	Mad Mad Mad Mad Mad Libs®
Christmas Fun Mad Libs®	Monster Mad Libs®
Cool Mad Libs®	More Best of Mad Libs®
Dance Mania Mad Libs®	Night of the Living Mad Libs®
Dear Valentine Letters Mad Libs®	Off-the-Wall Mad Libs®
Diva Girl Mad Libs®	The Original #1 Mad Libs®
Dude, Where's My Mad Libs®	Peace, Love, and Mad Libs®
Family Tree Mad Libs®	Pirates Mad Libs®
Fun in the Sun Mad Libs®	Prime-Time Mad Libs®
Girls Just Wanna Have Mad Libs®	P. S. I Love Mad Libs®
Goofy Mad Libs®	Rock 'n' Roll Mad Libs®
Grab Bag Mad Libs®	Slam Dunk Mad Libs®
Graduation Mad Libs®	Sleepover Party Mad Libs®
Happily Ever Mad Libs®	Son of Mad Libs®
Happy Birthday Mad Libs®	Sooper Dooper Mad Libs®
Haunted Mad Libs®	Spooky Mad Libs®
Holly, Jolly Mad Libs®	Straight "A" Mad Libs®
Kid Libs Mad Libs®	Upside Down Mad Libs®
Letters From Camp Mad Libs®	Vacation Fun Mad Libs®
Mad About Animals Mad Libs®	We Wish You a Merry Mad Libs®
Mad Libs® for President	Winter Games Mad Libs®
Mad Libs® from Outer Space	You've Got Mad Libs®

and many, many more!
Mad Libs® are available wherever books are sold.